This book belongs to

....

Walt Disney's

Donald Duck's Toy Train

Storybook Favourites

Reader's Digest Young Families

Walt Disney's
Donald Duck's Toy Train

Illustrations by The Walt Disney Studios
Adapted by Dick Kelsey and Bill Justice
from the motion picture *Out of Scale*
Story by Jane Werner

$\mathcal{D}$onald Duck had a new toy train in his garden, and it was a beauty, too.

It had a shiny black engine with a coal truck behind, where Donald rode. Because he was too big for the toy engine's cab.

Donald's train had a coach, a mail van, and a red guard's van, though none of his friends could go inside. Because it was a toy-sized train.

There was a little station beside the track – Canyonville, the station sign said. And around the station a little village spread, with houses and churches, and stores. Only nobody lived there, because it was too small. And that did seem too bad.

One day Donald was laying some new train track when he came up against a great big tree.

'This will have to go!' said Donald Duck. 'It's much too big for my toy train.'

So he had the big tree moved away.

Now up in that treetop was the cosy home of two chipmunks, Chip 'n' Dale. They were away at the time, gathering nuts for their winter food.

Soon they came back with great armloads of nuts, and got ready to climb to their home. But what was this? The tree was gone! They could scarcely believe their eyes.

In its place Donald Duck had put a toy-sized tree, just the size for his little toy train.

'But it's not big enough for a home for us!' cried Chip.

'No sir!' cried Dale.

Well, this was a problem. Where could they live?

The two sad chipmunks sat and thought. But that didn't get them anywhere.

So they started walking slowly down the railroad tracks.
Soon they came to the train, where Donald had left it.
'Looks like fun,' said Chip.
'Let's go for a ride,' said Dale.

So they hopped into the engine cab, which was just their size. They stoked up the little fire with a shovelful of coal. And away they chugged, down the track.

They roared through tunnels, up hill and down dale. It was a really wonderful ride.

Soon they came to the town, and they rang the engine bell and pulled on the brakes and stopped.

'Quite a town!' said Chip.

'Let's look around,' said Dale.

So they rattled the doors of the little stores. But no one was there to sell them anything.

They knocked at the doors of the little houses. But nobody answered their knocks.

One little door, though, swung open at their touch. So Chip 'n' Dale walked inside.

Inside the house they found chairs and lamps and tables and beds – all exactly chipmunk size.

So Chip 'n' Dale moved right in.

But not far away a danger lurked. It was Donald Duck. And Donald Duck was mad!

'Someone has stolen my train,' he fumed.

'Best toy train in the world!' he fussed. 'And it's probably wrecked by now. It isn't everyone who can manage a real little train like that.'

Just then he looked up and saw the train, parked at the station as neat as could be.

Near the train he found tiny footprints, leading straight to the little house.

Donald went to the window and peeked in. Chip 'n' Dale were curled up in bed, taking naps.

'Well, isn't that cute!' said Donald. 'What's more, they're just the right size!'

So Donald made friends with Chip 'n' Dale. He delivered tiny bottles of milk to their door and teeny loaves of bread.

And he let them drive his fine toy train, while he rode on a coach behind.

'It's much more fun,' said Donald happily, 'to play with folk who are just the right size!'

Walt Disney's Donald Duck's Toy Train is a *Disney Storybook Favourites* book

Walt Disney's Donald Duck's Toy Train, copyright © 1950, 2007 Disney Enterprises, Inc.
Story by Jane Werner. Illustrations adapted by Dick Kelsey and Bill Justice from the motion picture *Out of Scale.*

This edition was adapted and published in 2009 by
The Reader's Digest Association Limited
11 Westferry Circus, Canary Wharf, London E14 4HE

Editor: Rachel Warren Chadd
Designer: Louise Turpin
Design consultant: Simon Webb

® Reader's Digest, the Pegasus logo and Reader's Digest Young Families
are registered trademarks of
The Reader's Digest Association, Inc.

We are committed both to the quality of our products
and the service we provide to our customers.
We value your comments, so please do contact us on
08705 113366 or via our website at
www.readersdigest.co.uk
If you have any comments or suggestions
about the content of our books, email us at
gbeditorial@readersdigest.co.uk

Printed in China

A Disney Enterprises/Reader's Digest Young Families Book

ISBN 978 0 276 44481 4
Book code 641-040 UP0000-1
Oracle code 504400090H.00.24